My Buddy

MY BUDDY

Audrey Osofsky

illustrated by
Ted Rand

Henry Holt and Company • New York

Buddy is my best friend. He never gets mad at me. He never runs off to play with another boy. He always listens when I need someone to talk to.

Buddy is my golden retriever. He looks like the sun is always shining on him. When he sees me, his big brown eyes are sweet as a smile.

But Buddy is more than my friend. He's my arms and legs. He helps me do things I can't do by myself.

And I can't do a lot of things other kids can. I have a disease that makes my muscles weak. It's called muscular dystrophy.

Before Buddy, Mom and Dad helped me. Mike and other friends helped too. But friends sometimes get tired of helping. And I wanted to do things on my own.

Buddy was my wish come true. We met at a camp where Buddy was trained to help someone like me.

As a puppy, he was special. Loving and smart, he was chosen to be a Service Dog. Buddy was the star of puppy kindergarten. Top dog in his graduation class. In two years, Buddy had learned sixty commands.

I had to learn all the commands in two weeks. How to take care of Buddy, too.

It was hard. Much harder than I thought. We worked long hours and had tests every day. We called it "boot camp" because it was so tough. Like training in the Marines.

Over and over I practiced giving commands. It wasn't easy to make Buddy obey me. He acted like a kid who didn't pay any attention to his teacher.

Many times I'd get angry. Sometimes I cried. But I never gave up, even when I wanted to. I wanted Buddy more.

To help us bond, to feel that we belonged together, Buddy was leashed to my wrist all day and night. We had to do everything together. We slept together. We even took showers together!

I began to understand Buddy better. And myself, too. I had to believe I was a leader before Buddy would believe. After many days, my voice got stronger when I gave commands.

One day Buddy looked me in the eye—and obeyed. He learned to trust me, and I learned to trust him.

Then I graduated too, and we were a team.

WORKING DOG
DON'T TOUCH

Back home, Mike came over to meet my new friend.

"Don't pet him or give him snacks," I said. "Buddy doesn't eat on the job."

I told Mike about the sixty commands, but I just showed him a few.

"Up, light!" I commanded, and Buddy turned on the light. "Good boy!"

"Tug!" I commanded, and Buddy opened our front door.

"Let me try!" Mike said.

"Buddy only listens to me," I told him.

"You're lucky," Mike said.

We went to the shopping mall. I worried. Would Buddy keep his cool in a crowd?

Buddy was a pro. He pushed elevator buttons, fetched baseball cards from a high shelf, and kept me company at the barbershop.

Buddy's favorite job was at the pet store. He picked up a bag of doggy treats, gave the lady my dollar, and brought me the package with the change inside, wagging his tail.

TREATS

On the first day
of school, Buddy brought
me my clothes. Then he
fetched his blue-and-gold backpack.
He was ready to work.

Mom zipped up my lunch, notebook, and pencils in Buddy's pack and clipped it on his back. She gave me a hug. She wanted to give Buddy a hug too, but she couldn't, because he was working.

We rode to school together on our special bus. I wondered if kids would think it was weird to see a boy in a wheelchair with a dog in school. Maybe the teacher wouldn't want a dog in her class. Kids might play with him and he'd bark and act goofy.

MILK
MILK
MILK

At first, everyone wanted to pet Buddy.

"Buddy is a working dog, not a pet," the teacher explained. "His sign says 'Don't Touch' so he can keep his mind focused on his work."

Buddy fetched a pencil I had dropped, and kids said he was handy. Buddy brought me a book from the library shelf, and they said he was smart. In the lunchroom, Buddy retrieved my empty milk carton from the trash can, and they laughed and said he was funny.

Now the kids are used to a dog in school. When Buddy takes a nap, they step over him. He's just one of the guys.

My teacher likes Buddy too. He's the quietest one in the class.

After school, Buddy is ready for a run around our yard. On nice days, we play ball outside. I can't throw the ball very far, but Buddy doesn't care. He's just happy to play with me.

Sometimes Mike calls. Buddy picks up the phone and brings it to me.

"Come on over and play video games," Mike says.

We buzz over to Mike's house. Buddy rings the doorbell.

Buddy likes playing tee ball the best. I hit the Wiffle ball with a plastic bat and Buddy does the fielding. Whatever we do, we do together. We're a team.

Before Buddy, I didn't like to go places. People stared at me. Now people look at *us*—and ask about my dog.

Buddy is my best friend, I tell them.

At bedtime, I brush his shiny coat. Soon I'm tired and have to stop. Buddy licks my face. He knows I'm his best friend too.

"Up, switch!" I command, and Buddy turns off the light.

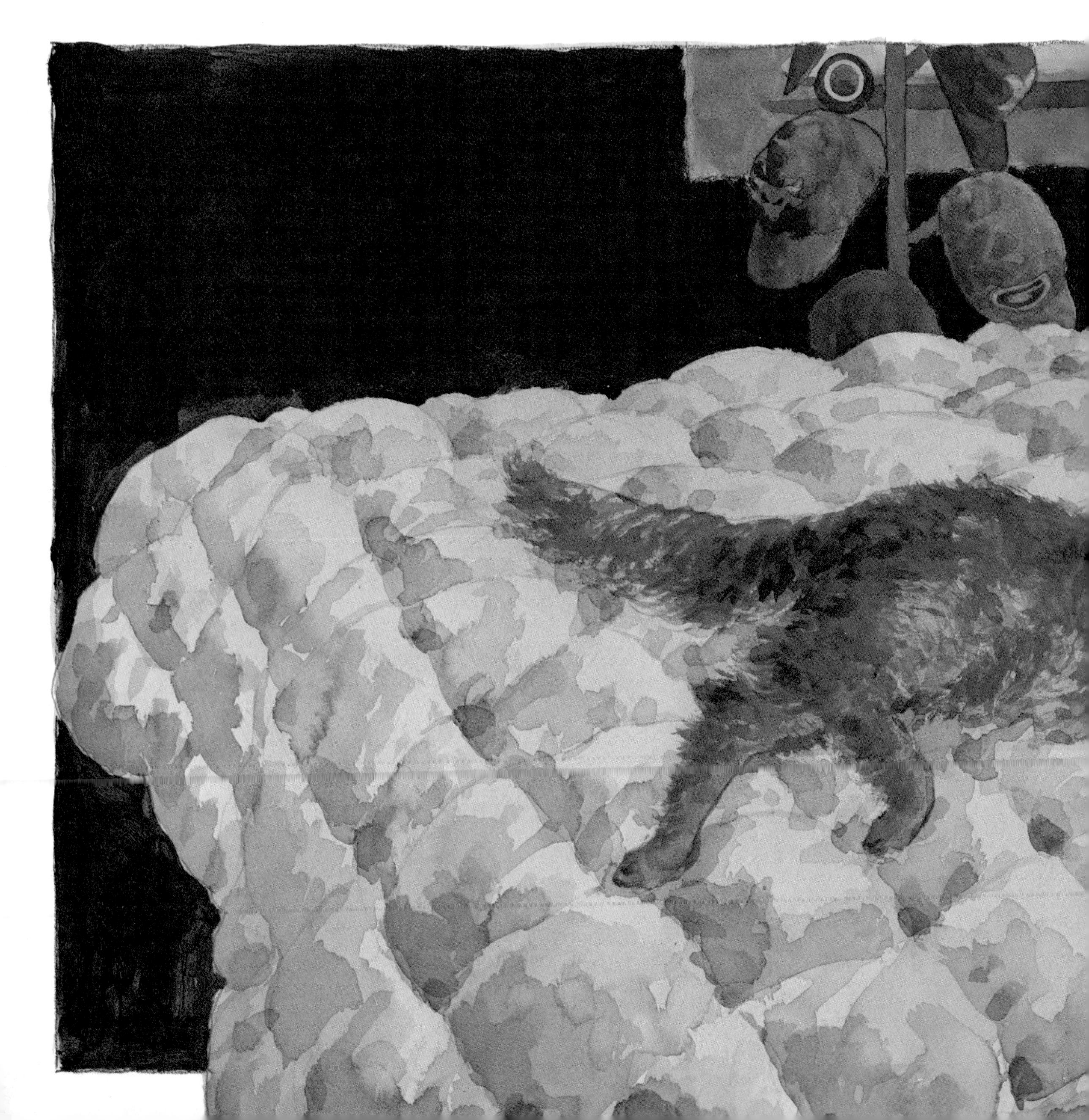

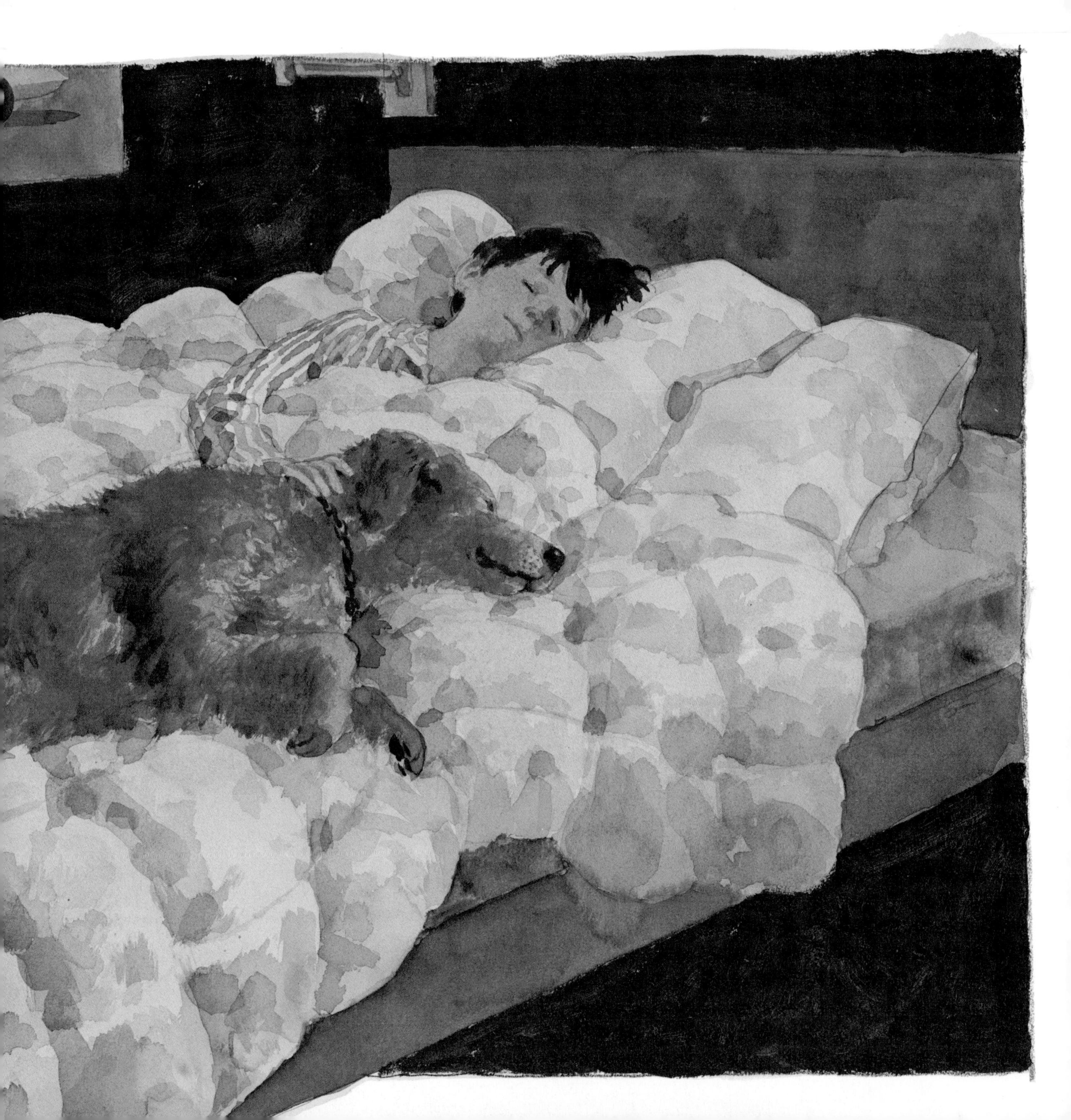

GIANTS

He gives me sloppy kisses.
I give him hugs back.
He's my Buddy.

To Scott LeRoy and his buddy, Rex,
and to happy memories of Rusty
—Audrey Osofsky

To John Lanspery, his family,
and his buddy, Newman,
and to the people at Canine Companions
for Independence at Santa Rosa, California,
with thanks for their help and inspiration
—Ted Rand

Henry Holt and Company, Inc. / *Publishers since 1866*
115 West 18th Street / New York, New York 10011

 Published in Canada by Fitzhenry & Whiteside Ltd.,
195 Allstate Parkway, Markham, Ontario L3R 4T8.

Library of Congress Cataloging-in-Publication Data
Osofsky, Audrey. My buddy / by Audrey Osofsky; illustrated by Ted Rand. Summary: A young boy with muscular dystrophy tells how he is teamed up with a dog trained to do things for him that he can't do for himself.
[1. Muscular dystrophy—Fiction. 2. Service dogs—Fiction. 3. Dogs—Fiction.] I. Rand, Ted, ill. II. Title.
PZ7.08347My 1992 [E]—dc20 92-3028

ISBN 0-8050-1747-X (hardcover): 10 9 8 7 6 5 4 3 2
ISBN 0-8050-3546-X (paperback): 10 9 8 7 6 5 4 3 2 1

First published in hardcover in 1992 by Henry Holt and Company, Inc.
First Owlet edition, 1994

Printed in the United States of America on acid-free paper. ∞